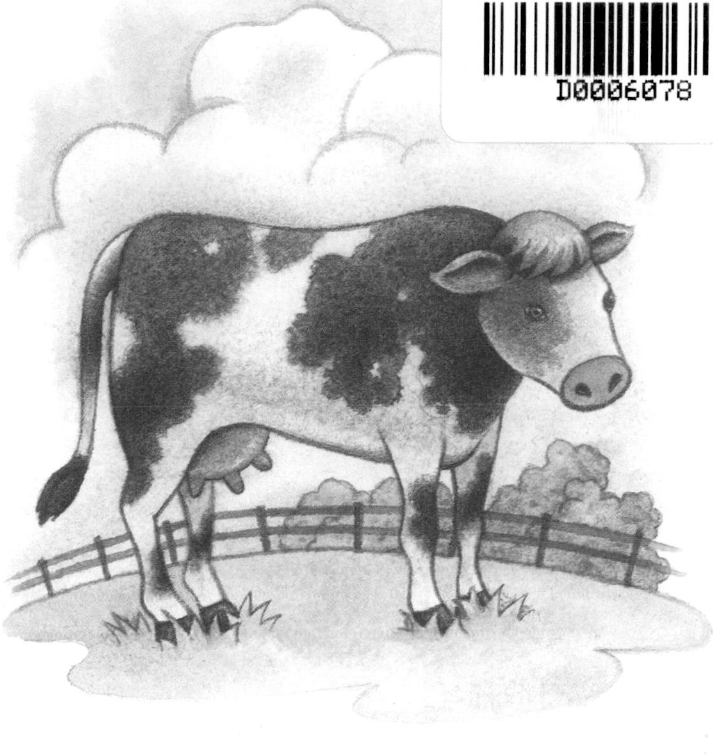

I see a cow.

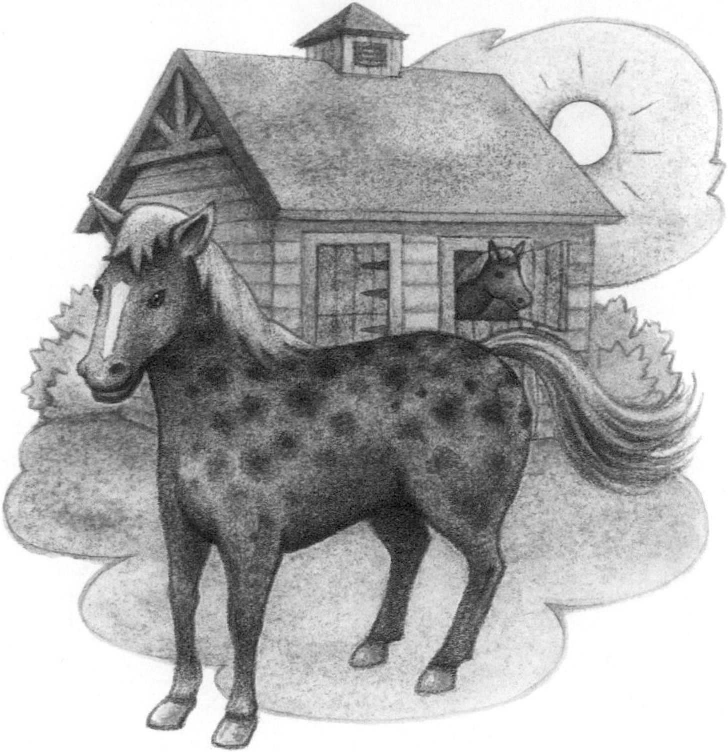

I see a horse.

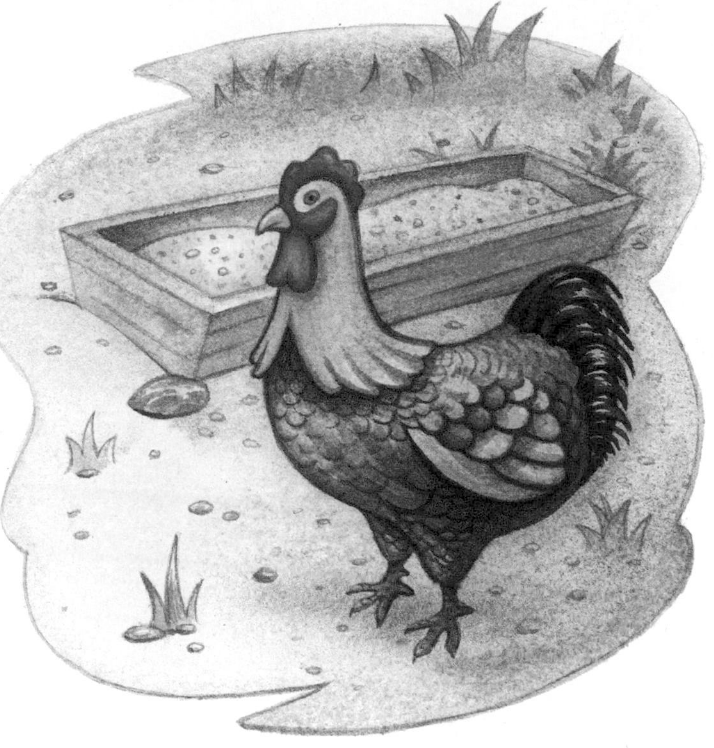

I see a hen.

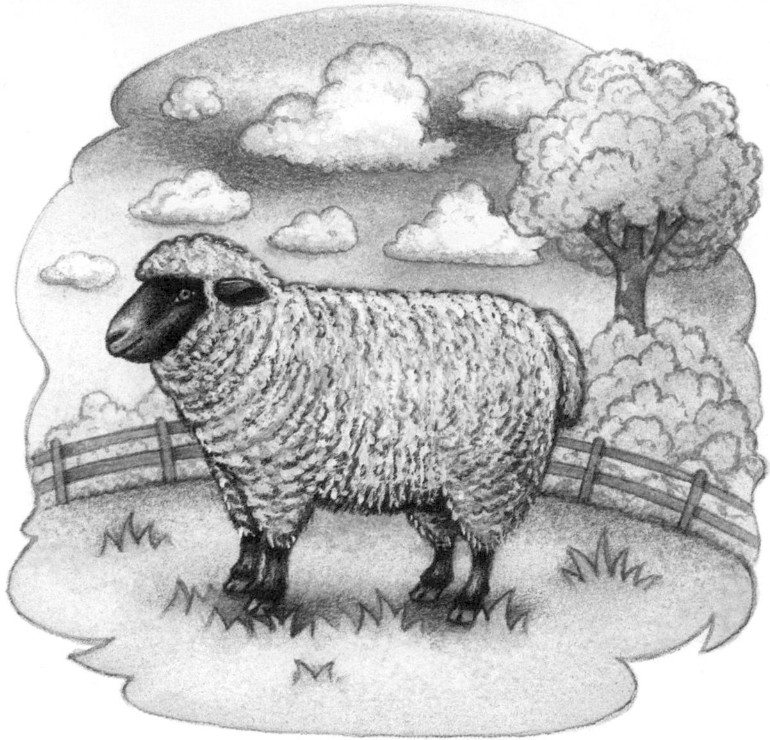

I see a sheep.

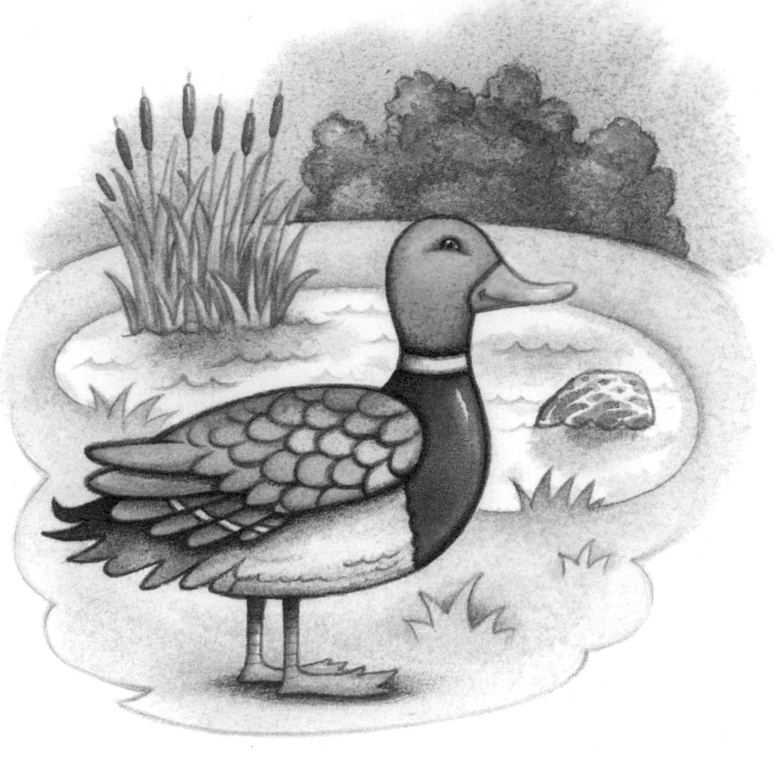

I see a duck.

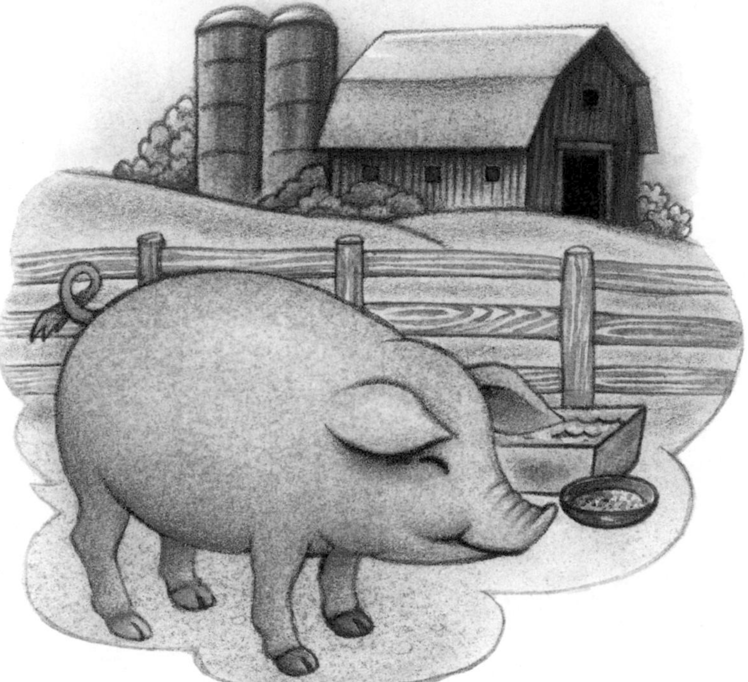

I see a pig.

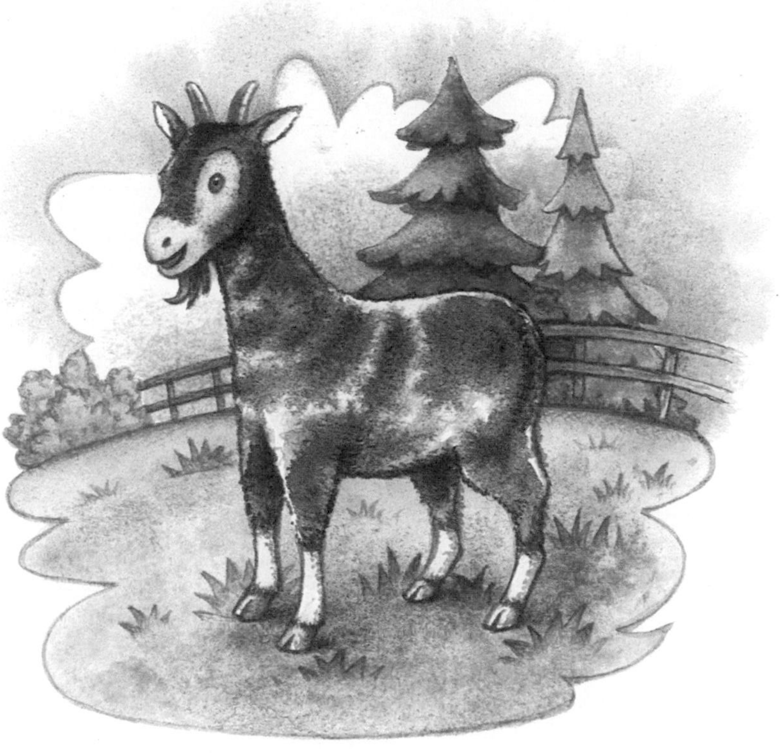

I see a goat.

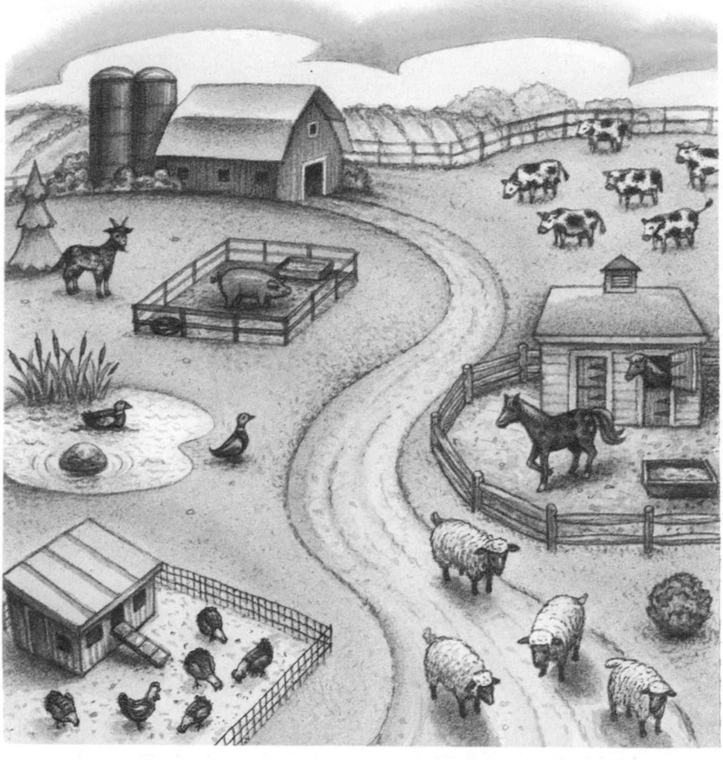

I see a farm.